I0566157

ONCE UPON A
TRAIN

BY

CRAIG RICE

Copyright © 2013 Read Books Ltd.
This book is copyright and may not be
reproduced or copied in any way without
the express permission of the publisher in writing

British Library Cataloguing-in-Publication Data
A catalogue record for this book is available from the
British Library

CONTENTS

CRAIG RICE.. 1

ONCE UPON A TRAIN 3

CRAIG RICE

Georgiana Ann Craig was born in Chicago in 1908. Her parents were highly neglectful of her, and Rice was raised by her aunt and uncle in Wisconsin. It is her uncle who has been credited with introducing the young Rice to mystery and speculative fiction by reading her the work of Edgar Allen Poe each evening.

During the late twenties and early thirties, Rice returned to Chicago and tried her hand at fiction-writing, music and acting, while earning a living writing for various local papers. She also worked as a radio writer and producer, and married three times. Her first hard-won success came in 1939, with the novel *Eight Faces at Three*, featuring a trio of protagonists – Jake Justus, Helene Brand and John Joseph Malone – who would go on to star in the majority of her fiction. Over the next decade Rice went on to produce between one and four mysteries a year, in a style that uniquely combined the hard-boiled detective tradition with surreal, screwball comedy. She had a devoted readership, and in 1946 became the first mystery writer to appear on the cover of *Time* magazine.

Rice's health deteriorated, however. In something of a mirroring of her often wild characters, she became a chronic alcoholic, and even attempted suicide more than once.

Having produced more than twenty novels, she died in Chicago before her fiftieth birthday.

ONCE UPON A TRAIN

CRAIG RICE AND STUART PALMER

'It was nothing, really,' said John J. Malone with weary modesty. 'After all, I never lost a client yet.'

The party in Chicago's famed Pump Room was being held to celebrate the miraculous acquittal of Stephen Larsen, a machine politician accused of dipping some thirty thousand dollars out of the municipal till. Malone had proved to the jury and to himself that his client was innocent – at least, innocent of that particular charge.

It was going to be a nice party, the little lawyer kept telling himself. By the way Larsen's so-called friends were bending their elbows, the tab would be colossal. Malone hoped fervently that his fee for services rendered would be taken care of today, before Larsen's guests bankrupted him. Because there was the matter of two months' back office rent . . .

'Thank you, I will,' Malone said, as the waiter picked up his empty glass. He wondered how he could meet the redhead at the next table, who looked sultry and bored in the midst of a dull family party. As soon as he got his money from Larsen he would start a rescue operation. The quickest way to make friends, he always said, was to break a hundred-dollar bill in a bar, and that applied even to curvaceous redheads in Fath models.

But where *was* Steve Larsen? Lolly was here, wearing her most angelic expression and a slinky gown which she overflowed considerably at the top. She was hinting that the party also celebrated a reconciliation between herself and Stevie; that the divorce was off. She had hocked her bracelet again, and Malone remembered hearing that her last show had closed after six performances. If she got her hand back into Steve's pocket, Malone reflected, goodbye to his fee of three grand.

He'd made elaborate plans for that money. They not only included the trip to Bermuda which he'd been promising himself for twenty years, but also the redhead he'd been promising himself for twenty minutes.

Others at the table were worrying too. 'Steve is late, even for him!' spoke up Allen Roth suddenly.

Malone glanced at the porcine paving-contractor who was rumoured to be Larsen's secret partner, and murmured, 'Maybe he got his dates mixed.'

'He'd *better* show,' Roth said, in a voice as cold as a grave-digger's shovel.

The little lawyer shivered, and realised that he wasn't the

only guest who had come here to make a collection. But he simply had to have that money. $3,000 – $30,000. He wondered, half-musing, if he shouldn't have made his contingent fee, say, $2,995. This way it almost looked like...

'What did you say about ten per cent, counsellor?' Bert Glick spoke up wisely.

Malone recovered himself. 'You misunderstood me. I merely said, "When on pleasure bent, never muzzle the ox when he treadeth out the corn." I mean rye.' He turned to look for the waiter, not solely from thirst. The little lawyer would often have been very glad to buy back his introduction to Bert Glick.

True, the city-hall hanger-on had been helpful during the trial. In fact, it had been his testimony as a prosecution witness that cinched the acquittal, for he had made a surprise switch on several moot points of the indictment. Glick was a private detective turned bail-bondsman, clever at tapping wires and dipping his spoon into any gravy that was being passed.

Glick slapped Malone on the back and said, 'If you knew what I know, you wouldn't be looking at your watch all the time. Because this ain't a coming-out party, it's a surprise party. And the surprise is that the host ain't gonna be here!'

Malone went cold – as cold as Allen Roth's grey eyes across

the table. 'Keep talking,' he said, adding in a whisper a few facts which Glick might not care to have brought to the attention of the district attorney.

'You don't need to be so nasty,' Glick said. He rose suddenly to his feet, lifting his glass. 'A toast! A toast to good ol' Stevie, our pal, who's taking the Super-Century for New York tonight, next stop Paris or Rio. And with him, my fine feathered friends, he's taking the dough he owes most of us, and a lot more too. Bon voyage!' The man absorbed the contents of his glass and slowly collapsed in his chair.

There was a sudden hullaballoo around the table. Malone closed his eyes for just five seconds, resigning himself to the certainty that his worst suspicions were true. When he opened his eyes again, the redhead was gone. He looked at his watch. There was still a chance of catching that New York train, with a quick stop at Joe the Angel's bar to borrow the price of a ticket. Malone rushed out of the place, wasting no time in farewells. Everybody else was leaving too. Finally, Bert Glick was alone, alone with the waiter and with the check.

As Malone had expected, Joe the Angel took a very dim view of the project, pointing out that it was probably only throwing good money after bad. But he handed over enough for a round trip, plus Pullman. By the time his cab had dumped him at the IC station, Malone had decided to settle for one-way. He needed spending money for the trip. There were poker games on trains.

Suddenly he saw the redhead! She was jammed in a crowd at the gate, crushed between old ladies, noisy sailors, and a bearded patriarch in the robes of the Greek Orthodox Church. She struggled with a mink coat, a yowling cat in a travelling case, and a caged parrot.

Malone leapt gallantly to her rescue, and for a brief moment was allowed to hold the menagerie, before a Redcap took over. The moment was just long enough for the lawyer to have his hand clawed by the irate cat, and for him and the parrot to develop a lifelong dislike. But he did hear the girl say, 'Compartment B in Car Ten, please.' And her warm grateful smile sent him racing off in search of the Pullman conductor.

Considerable eloquence, some trifling liberties with the truth, and a ten-dollar bill got him possession of the drawing-room next to a certain compartment. That settled, he paused to make a quick deal with a roving Western Union boy, and more money changed hands. When he finally swung aboard the already-moving train, he felt fairly confident that the trip would be pleasant and eventful. And lucrative, of course. The minute he got his hands on Steve Larsen . . .

Once established in the drawing-room, Malone studied himself in the mirror, whistling a few bars of 'On the Wabash

Cannonball'. For the moment the primary target could wait. He was glad he was wearing his favourite Finchley suit, and his new green and lavender Sulka tie.

'A man of distinction,' he thought. True, his hair was slightly mussed, a few cigar ashes peppered his vest, and the Sulka tie was beginning to creep toward one ear, but the total effect was good. Inspired, he sat down to compose a note to Operation Redhead, in the next compartment. He knew it was the right compartment, for the parrot was already giving out with imitations of a boiler factory, assisted by the cat.

He wrote: *Lovely lady, let's not fight Fate. We were destined to have dinner together. I am holding my breath for your eyes. Your unknown admirer, JJM.* He poked the note under the connecting door, rapped lightly, and waited.

After a long moment the note came back, with an addition in a surprisingly precise hand. *Sir, you have picked the wrong girl. Besides, I had dinner in the Pump Room over an hour ago, and so I believe did you.*

Undaunted, Malone whistled another bar of the song. Just getting any answer at all was half the battle. So she'd noticed him in the Pump Room! He sat down and wrote swiftly, *Please, an after-dinner liqueur with me, then?*

This time the answer was: *My dear sir: MY DEAR SIR!* But the little lawyer thought he heard sounds of feminine laughter, though of course it might have been the parrot. He sat back, lit a fresh cigar, and waited. They were almost to Gary now, and if the telegram had got through . . .

It had, and a messenger finally came aboard with an armful of luscious *Gruss von Teplitz* roses. Malone intercepted him long enough to add a note which really should be the clincher. *To the Rose of Tralee, who makes all other women look like withered dandelions. I'll be waiting in the club car. Faithfully, John J. Malone.* That was the way, he told himself happily. Don't give her a chance to say No again.

After a long and somewhat bruising trip through lurching Pullman cars, made longer still because he first headed fore instead of aft, Malone finally sank into a chair in the club-car lounge, facing the door. Of course, she would take time to arrange the roses, make a corsage out of a couple of buds, and probably shift into an even more startling gown. It might be quite a wait. He waved at the bar steward and say, 'Rye, please, with a rye chaser.'

'You mean rye with a beer chaser, Mista Malone?'

'If you know my name, you know enough not to confuse me. I mean beer with a rye chaser!' When the drink arrived Malone put it where it would do the most good, and then for lack of anything better to do fell to staring in awed fascination at the lady who had just settled down across the aisle.

She was a tall, angular person who somehow suggested

a fairly well-dressed scarecrow. Her face seemed faintly familiar, and Malone wondered if they'd met before. Then he decided that she reminded him of a three-year-old who had winked at him in the paddock at Washington Park one Saturday and then run out of the money.

Topping the face – as if anything could – was an incredible headpiece consisting of a grass-green crown surrounded by a brim of nodding flowers, wreaths, and ivy. All it seemed to need was a nice marble tombstone.

She looked up suddenly from her magazine. 'Pardon me, but did you say something about a well-kept grave?' Her voice reminded Malone of a certain Miss Hackett who had talked him out of quitting second-year high school. Somehow he found himself strangely unable to lie to her.

'Madam, do you read minds?'

'Not minds, Mr Malone. *Lips*, sometimes.' She smiled. 'Are you really *the* John J. Malone?'

He blinked. 'How in the – oh, of course! The *magazine*! Those fact detective sheets *will* keep writing up my old cases. Are you a crime-story fan, Mrs—?'

'Miss Hildegarde Withers, schoolteacher by profession and meddlesome old snoop by avocation, at least according to the police. Yes, I've read about you. You solve crimes and right wrongs, but usually by pure accident while chasing through saloons after some young woman who is no better than she should be. Are you on a case now?'

'Working my way through the second bottle,' he muttered, suddenly desperate. It would never do for the redhead to come in and find him tied up with this character.

'I didn't mean that kind of a case,' Miss Withers explained. 'I gather that even though you've never lost a client, you have mislaid one at the moment?'

Malone shivered. The woman had second sight, at least. He decided that it would be better if he went back through the train and met the Rose of Tralee, who must certainly be on her way here by this time. He could also keep an eye open for Steve Larsen. With a hasty apology he got out of the club car, pausing only to purchase a handy pint of rye from the bar steward, and started on a long slow prowl of mile after mile of wobbling, jerking cars. The rye, blending not unpleasantly with the champagne he had taken on earlier, made everything a little hazy and unreal. He kept getting turned around and blundering into the long-deserted diner. Two or three times he bumped into the Greek Orthodox priest with the whiskers, and similarly kept interrupting four sailors shooting craps in a men's lounge.

But – no redhead. And no Larsen. Finally the train stopped–could it be Toledo already? Malone dashed to the vestibule and hung over the step, to make sure that Steve didn't disembark. When they were moving again he resumed his pilgrimage, though by this time he had resigned himself to the fact that he was being stood up by the Rose of Tralee. At last, he turned mournfully back toward where his own lonesome cubicle ought to be – and then suddenly found himself back in the club car!

No redheaded Rose. Even The Hat had departed, taking her copy of *Official Fact Detective Stories* with her. The car was deserted except for a bridge game going on in one corner and a sailor – obviously half-seas over – who was drowsing in a big chair with a newspaper over his face.

The pint was empty. Malone told the steward to have it buried with full military honours, and to fetch him a cheese on rye. 'On second thought, skip the cheese and make it just straight rye, please.'

The drink arrived, and with it a whispered message. There was a lady waiting down the corridor.

Malone emptied his glass and followed the steward, trying to slip him five dollars. It slipped right back. 'Thanks, Mister Malone, but I can't take money from an old classmate. Remember, we went through the last two years of Kent College of Law together?'

Malone gasped. 'Class of '25. And you're Homer – no *Horace* Lee Randolph. But—'

'What am I doing here? The old story. Didn't know my place, and got into Chicago southside politics. Bumped up against the machine, and got disbarred on a phoney charge of subornation of perjury. It could have been squared by handing a grand to a certain sharper at City Hall, but I didn't have the money.' Horace shrugged. 'This pays better than law, anyway. For instance, that lady handed me five dollars just to unlock the private lounge and tell you she's waiting to see you there.'

The little lawyer winced. 'She – was she a queer old maid in a hat that looked like she'd made it herself?'

'Oh, no. No hat.'

Malone breathed easier. 'Was she young and lovely?'

'My weakness is the Numbers game, but I should say the description is accurate.'

Humming 'But 'twas not her beauty alone that won me, oh, no, 'twas the truth', Malone straightened his tie and opened the door.

Lolly Larsen exploded in his face with all the power of a firecracker under a tin can. She grabbed his lapels and yelped: 'Well, where is the dirty—'

'Be more specific. Which dirty—?' Malone said, pulling himself loose.

'*Steve*, of course!'

'I don't know, but I still hope he's somewhere on this train. You joining me in the search? Nice to have your pretty face among us.'

Lolly had the face of a homesick angel. Her hair was exactly the colour of a twist of lemon peel in a glass of champagne brut, her mouth was an overripe strawberry, and her figure might have inspired the french bathing-suit, but her eyes were cold and strange as a mermaid's. 'Are you in this with Steve?' she demanded.

Malone said: 'In simple, one-syllable words that even you can understand – No!'

Lolly suddenly relaxed, swaying against him so that he got a good whiff of brandy, nail polish, and Chanel Number Five. 'I'm sorry. I guess I'm just upset. I feel so terribly helpless.' For Malone's money, she was as helpless as an eight-button rattlesnake. 'You see,' Lolly murmured, 'I'm partly to blame for Steve's running away. I should have stood by him at the trial, but I hadn't the courage. Even afterward – I didn't actually promise to come back to him, I just said I'd come to his party. I meant to tell him – in the Pump Room. So, please, please help me find him – so I can make him see how much we really *need* each other!'

Malone said, 'Try it again, and flick the eyelashes a little bit more when you come to "need each other".'

Lolly jerked away and called him a number of things, of which 'dirty little shyster' was the most complimentary. 'All right,' she finally said in a matter-of-fact tone. 'Steve's carrying a hundred grand, and you can guess how he got it. I

14

happen to know – Glick isn't the *only* one who's been spying on him since he got out of jail yesterday. I don't want Steve back, but I do want a fat slice for keeping my mouth shut. One word from me to the DA or the papers, and not even you can get him off.'

'Go on,' Malone said wearily. 'But you interest me in less ways than one.'

'Find Steve!' she told him. 'Make a deal and I'll give you ten per cent of the take. But work fast, because we're not the only ones looking for him. Steve doublecrossed everybody who was at that party this afternoon. He's somewhere on this train, but he's probably shaved off his moustache, or put on a fright-wig, or—'

Malone yawned and said, 'Where can I get in touch with you?'

'I couldn't get a reservation of any kind.' Her strange eyes warmed hopefully. 'But I hear you have a drawing-room?'

'Don't look at me in that tone of voice,' Malone said hastily. 'Besides, I snore. Maybe there'll be something available for you at the next stop.'

He was out of there and back in the club car before Lolly could turn on any more of the charm. He decided to have one for the road – the New York Central Road, and one for the Pennsy too. The sensible thing was to find Steve Larsen, collect his own hard-earned fee, and let Lolly alone. Her offer of ten per cent of the blackmail take touched on a sore spot.

Malone began to work his way through the train again, this time desperately questioning porters. The worst of it was, there was nothing remarkable about Larsen's appearance except curly hair, which he'd probably had straightened and dyed, a moustache that could have been shaved off, and a briefcase full of money, which he'd probably hidden. In fact, the man was undoubtedly laughing at everybody from behind a false set of whiskers.

Such were Malone's thoughts as he suddenly came face to face again with the Greek Orthodox priest, who stared past him through thick, tinted spectacles. The little lawyer hesitated and was lost. Throwing caution to the winds, he yanked vigorously at the beard. But it was an orthodox beard, attached in the orthodox manner. Its owner let loose a blast which just possibly might have been an orthodox Greek blessing. Malone didn't wait to find out.

His ears were still burning when he stepped into a vestibule and ran head on into Miss Hildegarde Withers. He nodded coldly and started past her.

'Ah, go soak your fat head!'

Malone gasped.

'It's the parrot,' Miss Withers explained, holding up the caged monstrosity. 'It's been making such a racket that I'm taking it to the baggage car for the night.'

'Where – where did you get that – bird?' Malone asked weakly.

'Why, Sinbad is a legacy from the aunt whose funeral I just went back to attend. I'm taking him back to New York with me.'

'New York!' Malone moaned. 'We'll be there before I find that—'

'You mean that Mr Larsen?' As he stood speechless, she went briskly on. 'You see, I happened to be at a family farewell party at the table next to yours in the Pump Room, and my hearing is very acute. So, for that matter, is my eyesight. Has it occurred to you that Larsen may be wearing a disguise of some sort?'

'That it has,' admitted Malone sadly, thinking of the Greek priest.

The schoolteacher lowered her voice. 'You remember that when we had our little chat in the club car some time ago, there was an obviously inebriated sailor dozing behind a newspaper?'

'There's one on every train,' Malone said. 'One or more.'

'Exactly. Like Chesterton's postman, you never notice them. But somehow that particular sailor managed to stay intoxicated without ordering a single drink or nipping at a private bottle. More than that, when you suddenly left he poked his head out from behind the paper and stared after you with a very odd expression, rather as if he suspected you had leprosy. I couldn't help noticing—'

'Madam, I love you,' the lawyer said fervently. 'I love you because you remind me of Miss Hackett back in Dorchester High, and because of your hat, and because you are sharper than a tack.'

Miss Withers sniffed, but it was a mollified sniff. 'Sorry to interrupt, but that same sailor entered our car just as I left it with the parrot. I just happened to look back, and I rather think he was trying the door of your drawing-room.'

Malone clasped her hand fondly. Unfortunately it was the hand that held the cage, and the parrot took advantage of the long-awaited opportunity to nip viciously at his thumb. 'Thank you so very much – some day I'll wring your silly neck,' was Malone's sincere but somewhat garbled exit-line.

'Go boil your head in lard,' the bird screamed after him.

The maiden schoolteacher sighed. 'Come on, Sinbad, you're going into durance vile. And I'm going to retire to my lonely couch, drat it all.' She looked wistfully over her shoulder. 'Some people have all the fun!'

But twelve cars, ten minutes, and four drinks later, Malone was lost again. A worried porter was saying, 'If you could only remember your car number, sah?' A much-harassed Pullman conductor added, 'If you'd just show us your ticket stub, we'd locate you.'

'You don't need to locate *me*,' Malone insisted. 'I'm right here.'

'Maybe you haven't got a stub.'

'I have so a stub. It's in my hatband.' Crafty as an Indian guide, Malone backtracked them unerringly to his drawing-room. 'Here's the stub – now where am I?'

The porter looked out the window and said, 'Just coming into Altoona, sah.'

'They lay in the wreck when they found them, they had died when the engine had fell . . .' sang Malone happily. But the conductor winced and said they'd be going.

'You might as well,' Malone told him. 'If neither of you can sing baritone.'

The door closed behind them, and a moment later a soft voice called, 'Mr Malone?'

He stared at the connecting door. The Rose of Tralee, Malone told himself happily. He adjusted his tie, and tried the door. Miraculously, it opened. Then he saw that it was Miss Hildegarde Withers, looking very worried, who stared back at him.

Malone said, 'What have you done with my redhead?'

'If you refer to my niece Joannie,' the schoolteacher said sharply, 'she only helped me get my stuff aboard and rode as far as Englewood. But never mind that now. I'm in trouble.'

'I knew there couldn't be two parrots like that on one train,' Malone groaned. 'Or even in one world.'

'There's worse than parrots on this train,' snapped Miss Withers. 'This man Larsen you were looking for—'

The little lawyer's eyes narrowed. 'Just what is your interest in Larsen?'

'None whatever, except that he's here in my compartment. It's very embarrassing, because he's not only dead, he's *undressed!*'

'Holy St Vitus!' gulped Malone. 'Quiet! Keep *calm*. Lock your door and *don't* talk!'

'My door is locked, and who's talking?' the schoolteacher stepped aside and Malone peered gingerly past her. The speed with which he was sobering up probably established a new record. It was Larsen, all right. He was face down on the floor, dressed only in black shoes, blue socks, and a suit of long underwear. There was also a moderate amount of blood.

At last Malone said hoarsely, 'I suspect foul play!'

'Knife job,' said Miss Withers with professional coolness. 'From the back, through the *latissimus dorsi*. Within the last twenty minutes, I'd say. If I hadn't had some difficulty in convincing the baggage men that Sinbad should be theirs for the night, I might have walked in on the murderer at work.'

She gave Malone a searching glance. 'It wasn't *you*, by any chance?'

'Do you think I'd murder a man who owed me $3,000?' Malone demanded indignantly. He scowled. 'But a lot of people are going to jump to that conclusion. Nice of you not to raise an alarm.'

She sniffed. 'You didn't think I'd care to have a man – even a dead man – found in my room in this state of undress? Obviously, he hasn't your money on his person. So – what is to be done about it?'

'I'll defend you for nothing,' John J. Malone promised. 'Justifiable homicide. Besides, you were framed. He burst in upon you and you stabbed him in defence of your honour . . .'

'*Just* a minute! The corpse was *your* client. You've been publicly asking for him all through the train. I'm only an innocent bystander.' She paused. 'In my opinion, Larsen was lured to your room purposely by someone who had penetrated his disguise. He was stabbed, and dumped here. Very clever, because if the body had been left in your room, you could have got rid of it or claimed that you were framed. But this way, to the police mind at least, it would be obvious that you did the job and then tried to palm it off on the nearest neighbour.'

Malone sagged weakly against the berth. His hand brushed

against the leather case, and something slashed viciously at his fingers. 'But I thought you got rid of that parrot!' he cried.

'I did,' Miss Withers assured him. 'That's Precious in his case. A twenty-pound Siamese, also part of my recent legacy. Don't get too close, the creature dislikes train travel and is in a foul temper.'

Malone stared through the wire window and said, 'It's father must have been either a bobcat or a buzz saw.'

'My aunt left me her mink coat, on condition that I take both her pets,' Miss Withers explained wearily. 'But I'm beginning to think it would be better to shiver through these cold winters. And speaking of cold – I'm a patient woman, but not very. You have one minute, Mr Malone, to get your dead friend out of here!'

'He's no friend of mine, dead or alive,' Malone began. 'And I suggest—'

There was a heavy knocking on the corridor door. 'Open up in there!'

'Say something!' whispered Malone. 'Say you're undressed!'

'You're undressed – I mean, I'm undressed,' she cried obediently.

'Sorry, ma'am,' a masculine voice said on the other side of the door. 'But we're searching this train for a fugitive from justice. Hurry, please.'

'Just a minute,' sang out the schoolteacher, making frantic gestures at Malone.

The little lawyer shuddered, then grabbed the late Steve Larsen and tugged him through the connecting door into his drawing-room. Meanwhile, Miss Withers cast aside maidenly modesty and tore pins from her hair, the dress from her shoulders. Clutching a robe around her, she opened the door a crack and announced, 'This is an *outrage!*'

The train conductor, a Pullman conductor, and two Altoona police detectives crowded in, ignoring her protest. They pawed through the wardrobe, peered into every nook and cranny.

Miss Withers stood rooted to the spot, in more ways than one. There was a damp brownish-red spot on the carpet, and she had one foot firmly holding it down. At last the delegation backed out, with apologies. Then she heard a feeble, imploring tapping on the connecting door, and John J. Malone's voice whispering, 'Help!'

The maiden schoolteacher stuck her head out into the corridor again, where the search-party was already waiting for Malone to open up. 'Oh, officer!' she cried tremulously, 'is there any danger?'

'No, ma'am.'

'Was the man you're looking for a burly, dark-complexioned

cut-throat with dark glasses and a pronounced limp in the left leg?'

'No, lady. Get lost, please, lady.'

'Because on my way back from the diner I saw a man like that. He leered, and then followed me through three cars.'

'The man we're looking for is an embezzler, not a mental case.' They hammered on Malone's door again. 'Open up in there!'

Over her shoulder Miss Withers could see the pale, perspiring face of John J. Malone as he dragged Steve Larsen back into her compartment again.

'But, officer,' she improvised desperately, 'I'm sure that the awful dark man who followed me was a distinct criminal type—' There was a reassuring whisper of 'Okay' from behind her, and the sound of a softly closing door. Miss Withers backed into her compartment, closed and locked the connecting door, and then sank down on the edge of her berth, trying to avoid the blankly staring eyes of the dead man.

Next door there was a rumble of voices, and then suddenly Malone's high tenor doing rough justice to 'Did Your Mother Come from Ireland?' The schoolteacher heard no more than the first line of the chorus before the jello in her knees melted completely. When she opened her eyes again, she saw Malone holding a dagger before her, and she very nearly fainted again.

'You were so right,' the little lawyer told her admiringly. 'It was a frame-up all right – but meant for me. *This* was tucked into the upholstery of my room. I sat on it while they were searching, and had to burst into song to cover my howl of anguish.'

'Oh, dear!' said Miss Withers.

He sat down beside her, patted her comfortingly on the shoulder, and said, 'Maybe I can shove the body out the window!'

'We're still in the station,' she reminded him crisply. 'And from what experience I've had with train windows, it would be easier to solve the murder than open one. Why don't we start searching for clues?'

Malone stood up so quickly that he rapped his head on the bottom of the upper berth. 'Never mind *clues*. Let's just find the murderer!'

'Just as easy as that?'

'Look,' he said. 'This train was searched at the request of the Chicago police because somebody – probably Bert Glick – tipped them off that Larsen and a lot of stolen money are on board. The word has got around. Obviously, somebody else knew – somebody who caught the train and did the dirty work. It's reasonable to assume that whoever has the money is the killer.'

There was a new glint in Miss Withers' blue-grey eyes. 'Go on.'

'Also, Larsen's ex-wife – or do I mean ex-widow? – is aboard. I saw her. She is a lovely girl whose many friends agree that she would eat her young or sell her old mother down the river into slavery for a fast buck.' He took out a cigar. 'I'll go next door and have a smoke while you change, and then we'll go look for Lolly Larsen.'

'I'm practically ready now,' the schoolteacher agreed. 'But take *that* with you!'

Malone hesitated, and then with a deep sigh reached down and took a firm grasp of all that was mortal of his late client. 'Here we go again!'

A few minutes later Miss Hildegarde Withers was following Malone through the now-darkened train. The fact that this was somebody else's problem never occurred to her. Murder, according to her tenets, was everybody's business.

Malone touched her arm as they came at last to the door of the club car. 'Here is where I saw Lolly last,' he whispered. 'She only got aboard at the last minute, and didn't have a reservation.' He pointed down the corridor. 'See that door, just this side of the pantry? It's a private lounge, used only for railroad officials or big-shots like governors or senators. Lolly bribed the steward to let her use it when she wanted to have a private talk with me. It just occurred to me that she might have talked him into letting her have it for the rest of the night. If she's still there—'

'Say no more,' Miss Withers cut in. 'I am a fellow-passenger, also without a berth, seeking only a place to rest my weary head After all, I have as much right in there as she has. But you will be within call, won't you?'

'If you need help, just holler,' he promised. Malone watched as the schoolteacher marched down the corridor, tried the lounge door gently, and then knocked. The door opened and she vanished inside.

The little lawyer had an argument with his conscience. It wasn't just that she reminded him of Miss Hackett, it was that she had become a sort of partner. Besides, he was getting almost fond of that equine face.

Oh, well, he'd be within earshot. And if there was anything in the inspiration which had just come to him, she wasn't in any real danger anyway. He went on into the bar. It was half-dark and empty now, except for a little group of men in Navy uniforms at the far end, who were sleeping sprawled and entangled like a litter of puppies.

'Sorry, Mister Malone, but the bar is closed,' a voice spoke up behind him. It was Horace Lee Randoph, looking drawn and exhausted. He caught Malone's glance toward the sleeping sailors and added, 'Against the rules, but the conductor said don't bother 'em.'

Malone nodded, and then said, 'Horace, we're old friends and classmates. You know me of old, and you know you can trust me. *Where did you hide it?*'

'Where did I hide what?'

'You know what!' Malone fixed the man with the cold and baleful eye he used on prosecution witnesses. 'Let me have it before it's too late, and I'll do my best for you.'

The eyes rolled. 'Oh, Lawdy! I knew I shouldn't a done it, Mista Malone! I'll show you!' Horace hurried on down through the car and unlocked a small closet filled with mops and brooms. From a box labelled Soap Flakes he came up with a paper sack. It was a very small sack to hold a hundred thousand dollars, Malone thought, even if the money was in big bills. Horace fumbled inside the sack.

'What's *that?*' Malone demanded.

'What would it be but the bottle of gin I sneaked from the bar? Join me?'

The breath went out of John J. Malone like air out of a busted balloon. He caught the doorknob for support, swaying like an aspen in the wind. It was just at that moment that they both heard the screams.

The rush of self-confidence with which Miss Hildegarde Withers had pushed her way into the lounge ebbed somewhat as she came face to face with Lolly Larsen. Appeals to sympathy, as from one supposedly stranded fellow passenger to another, failed utterly. It was not until the schoolteacher played her last card, reminding Lolly sharply that if there was any commotion the Pullman conductor would undoubtedly have them both evicted, that she succeeded in getting a toe-hold.

'Oh, *all right*!' snarled Lolly ungraciously. 'Only shut up and go to sleep.'

During the few minutes before the room went dark again, Miss Withers made a mental snapshot of everything in it. No toilet, no wardrobe, no closet. A small suitcase, a coat, and a handbag were on the only chair. The money must be somewhere in this room, the schoolteacher thought. There was a way to find out.

As the train flashed through the moonlit night, Miss Withers busily wriggled out of her petticoat and ripped it into shreds. Using a bit of paper from her handbag for tinder – and inwardly praying it wasn't a ten-dollar bill – she did what had to be done. A few minutes later she burst out into the corridor, holding her handkerchief to her mouth.

She almost bumped into one of the sailors who came lurching toward her along the narrow passage, and gasped, 'What do you want?'

He stared at her with heavy eyes, 'If it's any of your business, I'm looking for the latrine,' he said dryly.

When he was out of sight, Miss Withers turned and

peeked back into the lounge. A burst of acrid smoke struck her in the face. Now was the time. '*Fire!*' she shrieked.

Thick billows of greasy smoke flooded out through the half-open door. Inside, little tongues of red flame ran greedily along the edge of the seat where Miss Withers had tucked the burning rags and paper.

Down the corridor came Malone and Horace Lee Randolph, and a couple of startled bluejackets appeared from the other direction. Somebody tore an extinguisher from the wall.

Miss Winters grabbed Malone's arm. 'Watch her! She'll go for the money—'

The fire extinguisher sent a stream of foaming chemicals into the doorway just as Lolly Larsen burst out. Her mascara streaked down her face, already blackened by smoke, and her yellow hair was plastered unflatteringly to her skull. But she clutched a small leather case.

Somehow she tripped over Miss Withers' outstretched foot. The leather case flew across the corridor to smash against the wall, where it flew open, disclosing a multitude of creams, oils, and tiny bottles – a portable beauty parlour.

'She must have gone to sleep smoking a cigarette!' put in Miss Withers in loud clear tones. 'A lucky thing I was there to smell the smoke and give the alarm—'

But John J. Malone seized her firmly by the arm and

propelled her back through the train. 'It was a good try, but you can stop acting now. She doesn't have the money.' Back in her own compartment he confessed about Horace. 'I had a wonderful idea, but it didn't pay off. The poor guy's career as a lawyer was busted by a City Hall chiseller. If Larsen was the one, Horace might have spotted him on the train and decided to get even.'

'You were holding out on me,' said Miss Withers, slightly miffed.

Malone unwrapped a cigar and said, 'If anybody finds that money, I want it to be me. Because I've got to get my fee out of it or I can't even get back to Chicago.'

'Perhaps you'll learn to like Manhattan,' she told him brightly.

Malone said grimly, 'If something isn't done soon, I'm going to see Manhattan through those cold iron bars.'

'We're in the same boat. Except,' she added honestly, 'that I don't think the inspector would go so far as to lock me up. But he does take a dim view of anybody who finds a body and doesn't report it.' She sighed. 'Do you think we *could* get one of these windows open?'

Malone smothered a yawn and said, 'Not in my present condition of exhaustion.'

'Let's begin at the beginning,' the schoolteacher said. 'Larsen invited a number of people to a party he didn't plan to attend. He sneaked on this train, presumably disguised in a Navy enlisted man's uniform. How he got hold of it—'

'He was in the Service for a while,' said the little lawyer.

'The murderer made a date to meet his victim in your drawing-room, hoping to set *you* up as the goat. He stuck a knife in him and then stripped him, looking for a money-belt or something.'

'You don't have to undress a man to find a money-belt,' Malone murmured.

'Really? I wouldn't know.' Miss Withers sniffed. 'The knife was then hidden in your room, but the body was moved in here. The money—' She paused and studied him searchingly. 'Mr Malone, are you sure you didn't—?'

'We plead not guilty and not guilty by reason of insanity,' Malone muttered. He closed his eyes for just five seconds' much-needed rest, and when he opened them a dirty-looking dawn was glaring in at him through the window.

'Good morning,' Miss Withers greeted him, entirely too cheerfully. 'Did you get any ideas while you were in dreamland?' She put away her toothbrush and added, 'You know, I've sometimes found that if a problem seems insoluble, you can sleep on it and sometimes your subconscious comes up with the answer. Sometimes it's even happened to me in a dream.'

'It does? It *has*?' Malone sat up suddenly. 'Okay. Burglars can't be choosers. Sleep and the world sleeps – I mean, I'll just stand watch for a while and you try taking a nap. Maybe you can dream up an answer out of your subconscious. But dream fast, lady, because we get in about two hours from now.'

But when Miss Withers had finally been comfortably settled against the pillows, she found that her eyelids stubbornly refused to stay shut.

'Try once more,' John J. Malone said soothingly. She closed her eyes obediently, and his high, whispering tenor filled the little compartment, singing a fine old song. It was probably the first time in history, Miss Withers thought, that anyone had tried to use 'Throw Him Down, McCluskey' as a lullaby, but she found herself drifting off . . .

Malone passed the time by trying to imagine what he would do with a hundred grand if he were the murderer. There must have been a desperate need for haste – at any moment, someone might come back to the murder room. The money would have to be put somewhere handy – some obvious place where nobody would ever think of looking, and where it could be quickly and easily retrieved when all was clear.

There was an angry growl from Precious in his cage. 'If you could only say something besides "Meeerow" and "Fssst"!' Malone murmured wistfully. 'Because you're the only witness. Now if it had been the parrot . . .'

At last he touched Miss Withers apologetically on the shoulder. 'Wake up, ma'am, we're coming into New York. Quick, what did you dream?'

She blinked, sniffed, and came wide awake. 'My dream? Why – I was buying a hat, a darling little sailor hat, only it had to be exchanged because the ribbon was yellow. But first I wore it out to dinner with Inspector Piper, who took me to a Greek restaurant and the proprietor was so glad to see us that he said dinner was on the house. But naturally we didn't eat anything because you have to beware of the Greeks when they come bearing gifts. His name was Mr Roberts. That's all I remember.'

'Oh, *brother!*' said John J. Malone.

'And there wasn't anyone named Roberts mixed up in this case, or anyone of Greek extraction, was there?' She sighed. 'Pure nonsense. I guess a watched subconscious never boils.'

The train was crawling laboriously up an elevated platform. 'A drowning man will grasp at a strawberry,' Malone said suddenly. 'I've got a sort of an idea. Greeks bearing gifts – that means look out for somebody who wants to give you something for nothing. And that something could include gratuitous information.'

She nodded. 'Perhaps someone planned to murder Larsen

aboard this train and wanted you aboard to be the obvious suspect.'

The train shuddered to a stop. Malone leapt up, startled, but the schoolteacher told him it was only 125th Street. 'Perhaps we should check and see who gets off.' She glanced out the window and said, 'On second thought, let's not. The platform is swarming with police.'

They were interrupted by the porter, who brushed off Miss Withers, accepted a dollar from the gallant Malone, and then lugged her suitcases and the pet container down to the vestibule. 'He'll be in your room next,' she whispered to Malone. 'What do we do now?'

'We think fast,' Malone said. 'The rest of your dream! The sailor hat with the wrong ribbon! And Mr Roberts—'

The door burst open and suddenly they were surrounded by detectives, led by a grizzled sergeant in plain clothes. Lolly Larsen was with them. She had removed most of the traces of the holocaust, her face was lovely and her hair was gleaming, but her mood was that of a dyspeptic cobra. She breathlessly accused Miss Withers of assaulting her and trying to burn her alive, and Malone of engineering Steve Larsen's successful disappearance.

'So,' said Malone. 'You wired ahead from Albany, crying copper?'

'Maybe she did,' said the sergeant. 'But we'd already been

contacted by the Chicago police. Somebody out there swore a warrant for Steve Larsen's arrest . . .'

'Glick, maybe?'

'A Mr Allen Roth, according to the teletype. Now, folks—'

But Malone was trying to pretend that Lolly, the sergeant, and the whole police department didn't exist. He faced Miss Withers and said, 'About that dream! It must mean a sailor under false colours. We already know that Larsen was disguised in Navy uniform . . .'

'Shaddap!' said the sergeant. 'Maybe you don't know, mister, that helping an embezzler to escape makes you an assessory after the fact.'

'*Acc*essory,' corrected Miss Withers firmly.

'If you want Larsen,' Malone said easily, 'he's next door in my drawing-room, wrapped up in the blankets.'

'Sure, sure,' said the sergeant, mopping his face. 'Wise guy, eh?'

'Somebody helped Larsen escape – escape out of this world, with a shiv through the – through the—?' Malone looked hopefully at Miss Withers.

'The *latissimus dorsi*,' she prompted.

The sergeant barked, 'Never mind the double-talk. Where is this Larsen?'

Then Lolly, who had pushed open the connecting door,

let out a thin scream like tearing silk. 'It *is* Steve!' she cried. 'It's Steve, and he's dead!'

Momentarily the attention of the Law was drawn elsewhere. 'Now or never,' said Miss Withers coolly. 'About the Mr Roberts thing – I just remembered that there was a play by that name a while back. All about sailors in the last war. I saw it, and was somewhat shocked at certain scenes. Their language – but anyway, I ran into a sailor just after I started that fire, and he said he was looking for the *latrine*. Sailors don't use Army talk – in "Mr Roberts" they called it *the head*.'

Suddenly the Law was back, very direct and grim about everything. Miss Withers gasped with indignation as she found herself suddenly handcuffed to John J. Malone. But stone walls do not a prison make, as she pointed out to her companion-in-crime. 'And don't you see? It means—'

'Madam, I am ahead of you. There was a *wrong* sailor aboard this train even after Larsen got his. The murderer must have taken a plane from Chicago and caught this train at Toledo. I was watching to see who got off, not who got on. The man penetrated Larsen's disguise—'

'In more ways than one,' the schoolteacher put in grimly.

'And then after he'd murdered his victim, he took Larsen's sailor suit and got rid of his own clothes, realising that nobody notices a sailor on a train! Madam, I salute your subconscious!' Malone waved his hand, magnificent even in chains. 'The defence rests! Officer, call a cop!'

The train was crawling into one of the tunnels beneath Grand Central station, and the harried sergeant was beside himself. 'You listen to Mr Malone,' Miss Withers told their captor firmly, 'or I'll hint to my old friend Inspector Oscar Piper that you would look well on a bicycle beat way out in Brooklyn!'

'Oh, no!' the unhappy officer moaned. 'Not *that* Miss Withers!'

'That Miss Withers,' she snapped. 'My good man, all we ask is that you find the real murderer, who must still be on this train. He's wearing a Navy uniform . . .'

'Lady,' the sergeant said sincerely, 'you ask the impossible. The train is full of sailors. Grand Central is full of sailors.'

'But this particular sailor,' Malone put in, 'is wearing the uniform of the man he killed. *There will be a slit in the back of the jumper* – just under the shoulder blade!'

'When the knife went in,' Miss Withers added. 'Hurry, man! The train is stopping.'

It might still have been a lost cause had not Lolly put in her five cents. 'Don't listen to that old witch!' she cried. 'Officer, you do your duty!'

The sergeant disliked being yelled at, even by blondes. 'Hold all of 'em – her too,' he ordered, and leapt out on the platform. He seized upon a railroad dick, who listened and then grabbed a telephone attached to a nearby pillar. Somewhere far off an alarm began to ring, and an emotionless voice spoke over the public address system . . .

In less than two minutes the vast labyrinth of Grand Central was alerted, and men in Navy uniforms were suddenly intercepted by polite but firm railroad detectives who sprang up out of nowhere. Only one of the sailors, a somewhat older man who was lugging a pet container that wasn't his, had any real difficulty. He alone had a narrow slit in the back of his jumper.

Bert Glick flung the leather case down the track and tried vainly to run, but there was no place to go. The container flew open, and Precious scooted. Only a dumb Siamese cat, as Malone commented later, would have abandoned a lair that had a hundred grand tucked under its carpet of old newspapers.

'And to think that I spent the night within reach of that dough, and didn't grab my fee!' said Malone.

But it developed that there was a comfortable reward for the apprehension of Steve Larson, alive or dead. Before John J. Malone took off for Chicago, he accepted an invitation for dinner at Miss Withers' modest little apartment on West 74th Street, arriving with four dozen roses. It was a good dinner, and Malone cheerfully put up with the screamed insults of Sinbad and the well-meant attentions of Talley, the apricot poodle. 'Just as long as the cat stays lost!' he said.

'Yes, isn't it odd that nobody has seen hide nor hair of Precious! It's my idea that he's waxing fat in the caverns beneath Grand Central, preying on the rats who are rumoured to flourish there. Would you care for another piece of pie, Mr Malone?'

'All I really want,' said the little lawyer hopefully, 'is an introduction to your redheaded niece.'

'Oh, yes, Joannie. Her husband played guard for Southern California, and he even made all-American,' Miss Withers tactfully explained.

'On second thought, I'll settle for coffee,' said John J. Malone.

Miss Withers sniffed, not unsympathetically.

www.ingramcontent.com/pod-product-compliance
Lightning Source LLC
Chambersburg PA
CBHW022156260626
47155CB00018B/2267